Disney's

Robin Hood
Saves the Day

GROLIER
BOOK CLUB EDITION

First American Edition. Copyright © 1980 by The Walt Disney Company.
All rights reserved under International and Pan-American Copyright Conventions.
Published in the United States by Random House, Inc., New York,
and simultaneously in Canada by Random House of Canada Limited, Toronto.
Originally published in Denmark as ROBIN HOOD SLAR TIL IGEN
by Gutenberghus Baldene, Copenhagen.
Copyright © 1979 by Walt Disney Productions
ISBN: 0-394-84454-8 (trade)   0-394-94454-2 (lib. bdg.)
Manufactured in the United States of America
                         F G H I J K   6 7 8 9

In the little town of Nottingham,
the people were very worried.

Evil Prince John would soon be collecting
tax money from them again.

But they had no more money to give.

"If we do not pay the money," said Mrs. Owl, "we will go to jail."

"We need Robin Hood," said Mrs. Rabbit. "He would know what to do."

Inside the castle, Prince John sat playing with his gold coins. He loved gold more than anything else in the world.

He called for his adviser, Sir Hiss. "I need more gold!" he said to Sir Hiss.

"S-s-sire, the people have no more gold to give you," said Sir Hiss.

"Nonsense!" shouted the prince.
Then he called for the sheriff.
"Go to the town and collect
more taxes," he said.

So the sheriff went to the town.

The people in the town gave him the few
coins they had left.

Even little Skippy Rabbit gave money
to the sheriff.

He gave the gold coin
he had gotten
for his birthday.

Mr. Dog paid taxes, too.

The sheriff found the coins
Mr. Dog had hidden inside
the bandages on his broken leg.

Mr. and
Mrs. Owl
each gave
their last
gold coin.
But the
sheriff
said it was
not enough.

The sheriff had to find more gold
for Prince John.

He went to the church.

Inside, he found a coin in the poor box
and took it for Prince John.

"That money is for the poor!" said
Friar Tuck. "Please do not take it."

Friar Tuck was a kind man who always
tried to help the people of Nottingham.

"No one can refuse to pay taxes!" said
the sheriff. "You will hang for this!"

The sheriff marched Friar Tuck off to the castle dungeon.

One of his men, Trigger the buzzard, helped guard Friar Tuck along the way.

But the sheriff still did not have enough
gold for Prince John.

So he arrested many of the people of Nottingham
and put them in jail, too.

After a few days in jail, the people would
tell him where there was more gold.

Meanwhile, Robin Hood and his friend
Little John were hiding deep in Sherwood
Forest, near the town of Nottingham.

They were hiding because they were outlaws.

Robin Hood had stolen Prince John's
gold several times.

Each time Robin stole the gold,
he gave it back
to the people
of the town.

The people loved Robin Hood and Little John.
But Prince John hated them and wanted
to destroy them.
So the outlaws stayed hidden in Sherwood Forest.

On the day that
Friar Tuck was put
in jail, Skippy Rabbit
went to the forest
to find Robin Hood.

He told Robin and
Little John that
Friar Tuck was going
to be hung
the next morning.

"Prince John has gone too far," said Little John.
"We must teach him a lesson," said Robin Hood.

Robin and Little John
needed some disguises.

They each dressed up like a beggar.
Then they started off for Nottingham.
"Good luck!" said
Skippy Rabbit.

The Sheriff of Nottingham was outside
Prince John's castle, testing the new
hanging noose.

Trigger and his buzzard cousin, Nutsy,
were helping the sheriff.

Robin Hood and Little John walked up
to them.

The sheriff did not know who they were.

"Who is going to be hung?" asked Robin Hood.

"Friar Tuck," said the sheriff. "Because he
would not pay his taxes."

"Robin, this is terrible," said Little John in a whisper. "What are we going to do?"

"Do not worry," said Robin Hood. "I have a plan."

Then Robin whispered his secret plan
to Little John.

"Move along, you beggars," said the sheriff.
"We have important work to do."

That night, the sheriff
went to Friar Tuck's cell.
The poor friar was
in heavy chains.
"Good night, Friar,"
said the sheriff. "You
hang in the morning."
But Friar Tuck
was hoping that
Robin Hood would
save him.

The sheriff went to his office in
the castle dungeon and sat down.
    He was feeling very proud of himself.

    Then Trigger came to give him a report.
    "It is nine o'clock at night and all
is well," said Trigger.
    "Good," said the sheriff. "That means
I can take a little nap."

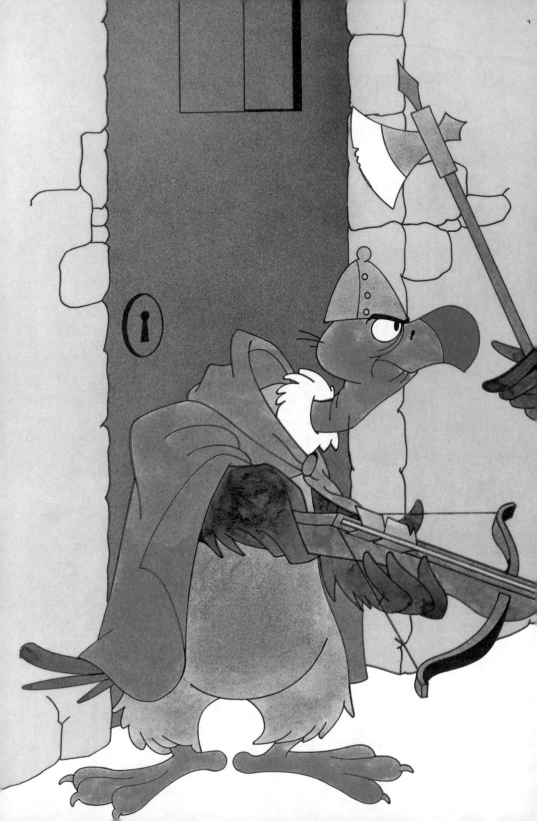

The sheriff fell sound asleep.
Trigger and Nutsy guarded the jail.
Several hours passed.

At midnight, Nutsy made the rounds
of the jail.

"Twelve o'clock and all is well!"
he shouted.

"Be quiet!" said Trigger. "We
must not wake the sheriff."

Nutsy walked on down the halls
of the dungeon.
Suddenly two hands reached
out and grabbed him.

It was Robin Hood!

After Robin grabbed Nutsy, he took off
Nutsy's cloak.

Then Little John tied Nutsy up.

Robin dressed himself in Nutsy's cloak.

Then he put on a nose that looked like Nutsy's nose.

It was a wonderful disguise.

Robin looked just like Nutsy.

"One o'clock in the morning and all is well," said Robin Hood in a loud voice.

He used a voice that sounded just like Nutsy's.

Trigger heard Robin calling out.

He thought he was hearing his cousin, Nutsy.

"Nutsy makes a lot of noise," he said to himself.

Then he walked on down the halls of the dungeon.

In the meantime, Little John tiptoed
into the sheriff's office.

The sheriff was still sound asleep.

Little John took the keys from
the sheriff's belt.

Then he went to Friar Tuck's cell.

Little John quickly
freed Friar Tuck.
Robin Hood stood
guard at the door.
"Oh, thank you,"
said Friar Tuck.
"But you must free
the other people, too."

Little John opened all the cells
in the dungeon.

"Oh, thank you, Little John," said
the people of Nottingham.

Robin Hood stood guard
in the hall outside.

"All is well!" he shouted.

Little John led the people
out of the castle.

Robin Hood waited until
the people had escaped.
Then he called out,
"Guards! Guards! Come
and catch Robin Hood!"

Trigger heard Robin calling.
But he thought it was his cousin, Nutsy.
"Quick!" he said to the Royal Rhinos.
"We must capture Robin Hood!"
The sheriff woke up in his dungeon office.

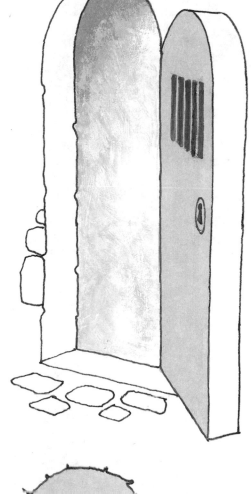

Trigger and the Royal
Rhinos ran into the dungeon.
When they all were inside,
Robin Hood locked
the door behind them.

Then Robin
ran upstairs
to Prince John's
bedroom.

Prince John was asleep in his bed.
Around him were all his bags of gold.
Sir Hiss was asleep there, too.
Robin Hood walked in quietly.

Without a sound,
Robin picked up
bag after bag
of gold.

He dropped each one
out the window.

Little John was waiting
down below.

He caught the bags of gold
as they fell.

Then he loaded them
onto a cart that
belonged to the people
of the town.

When Robin picked up
the last bag, he heard
PLINK! PLINK!
There was a hole in
the bottom of the bag!

Then Sir Hiss woke up and saw Robin Hood.
And he saw that the gold was gone.
"Sire!" he shouted.
"Call the guard!"
But the guard
was in jail.
The prince
was helpless.

Robin Hood
leaped from
the window—

and landed in the moat with a huge SPLASH!

Little Skippy Rabbit met him on the shore.
"Hurray, hurray!" he shouted. "You
are my hero, Robin Hood!"

Little John and Robin pulled
the cart full of gold
into the town.

Friar Tuck helped them divide
the gold into equal shares
for everyone.

Then Robin and Little John
went back to Sherwood Forest.

Prince John could not believe his eyes.
All his gold was gone!

"You idiot, Hiss!"
he shouted. "This is
all your fault!"

Sir Hiss could
do nothing.

"Yes-s-s, S-sire,"
he gasped.

It was all
the poor fellow
could say.